Sister Wish

Giselle Potter

Abrams Books for Young Readers

New York

For Pia and Izzy
and for my sister, Chloë

The illustrations in this book were made with watercolor and ink.

Cataloging-in-Publication Data has been applied for and
may be obtained from the Library of Congress.

ISBN 978-1-4197-4671-0

Text and illustrations copyright © 2021 Giselle Potter
Book design by Heather Kelly

Printed and bound in China
10 9 8 7 6 5 4 3 2 1

Abrams Books for Young Readers are available at special discounts when
purchased in quantity for premiums and promotions as well as fundraising or educational use.
Special editions can also be created to specification. For details, contact
specialsales@abramsbooks.com or the address below.

Abrams® is a registered trademark of Harry N. Abrams, Inc.

ABRAMS The Art of Books
195 Broadway, New York, NY 10007
abramsbooks.com

It must be nice to be so tall.

I grow out of all my favorite things and have to give them to you.

I wisH I wasn't missing my front teeth and that I had all my big teeth, like you.

I'm glad I have all my teeth.
But you still get presents
from the Tooth Fairy!

Well I wish I was a bird
who could soar through the sky!

...But a bird probably wishes it was a fish who could dive deep into the bottom of the ocean.

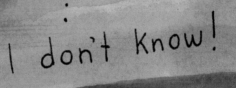

A fish probably wishes it had legs
and could gallop like a horse!

And a horse wishes it could get a ride instead of always being ridden on.

See, everyone wants to be someone else sometimes.

Sometimes...

I wish I could make people laugh like you do!

And I wish I could dress up in costumes whenever I want.

Oh, but you can do that if you want to!

And anyway, if there were two of me and none of you,

there would be no little sister to give piggyback rides to.

or do my famous
wiggle dance!

And if there were two of ME and none of YOU,

there would be no one to teach me how to whistle or do cartwheels,

or read me
stories at night.

. . . . . Or tell you about the things you don't know.

So,
. . . . . it's best if there is one of you
and one of me, right?

Right !